Sleepy Head! Sleepy Head!

Written by: Willie Nelson

Dedication:

To all my children, who are slow to start their mornings. Thank you for the inspiration for this story, my "Sleepy Heads."

Paperback: 979-8-218-04627-9

First paperback edition September 2022.

Sleepy Head! Sleepy Head!
It's time for you to get out of bed.
The morning sun is in the sky.
So wipe the sleep from your eyes!

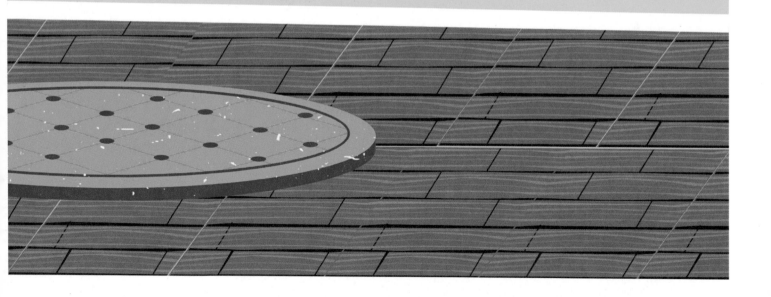

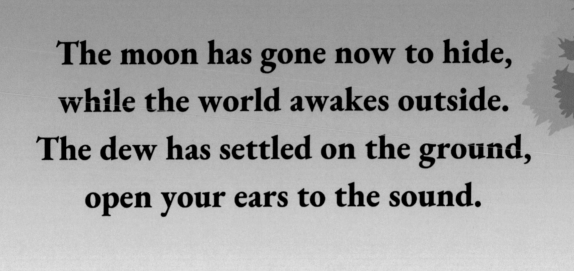

The moon has gone now to hide,
while the world awakes outside.
The dew has settled on the ground,
open your ears to the sound.

The birds have all began to sing,
while to your dreams you still tightly cling.

Sleepy Head! Sleepy Head!
Why are you still in your bed?

It's time for you to start your day.
The world is ready for you to
come out and play.

There are so many things for you to see.
The squirrels are jumping through the trees.
Bunnies have begun to jump around.
While raccoons and owls are no longer found.

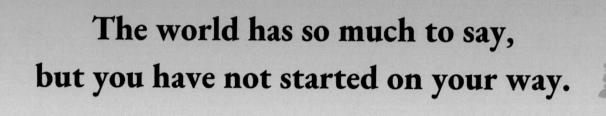

The world has so much to say,
but you have not started on your way.

Sleepy Head! Sleepy Head!
I'm going to carry you out of bed.

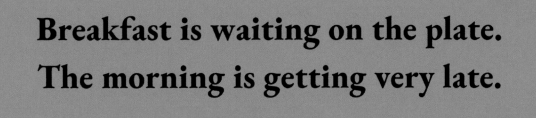

Breakfast is waiting on the plate.
The morning is getting very late.

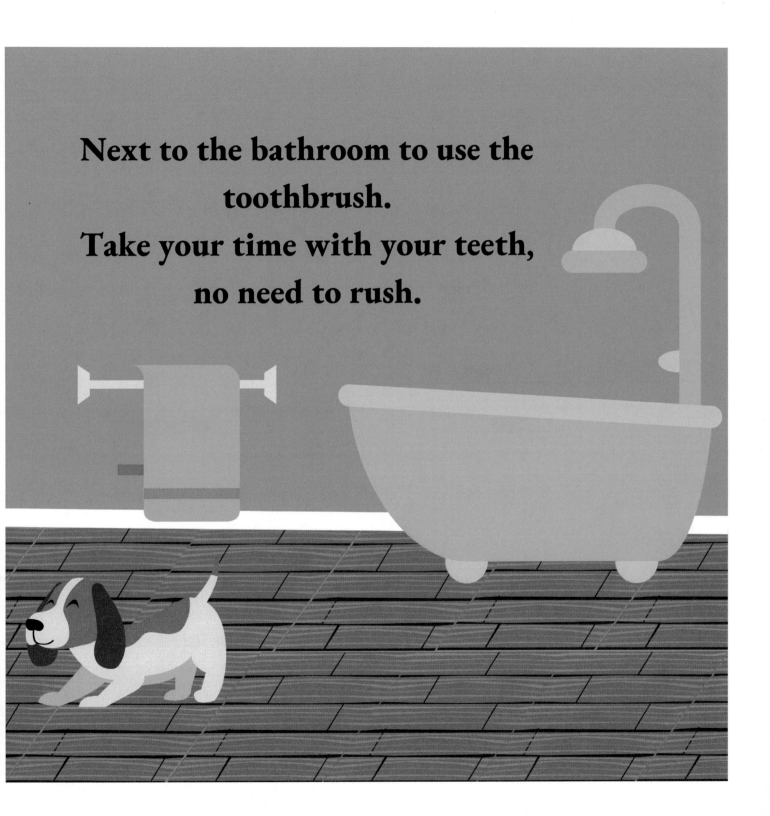

Next to the bathroom to use the toothbrush.
Take your time with your teeth, no need to rush.

**Finish up downstairs
with a kiss on the nose.**

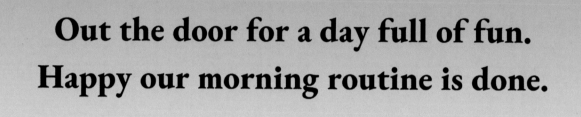

Out the door for a day full of fun.
Happy our morning routine is done.

Good Morning!
My Sleepy Head!

Made in the USA
Middletown, DE
10 August 2022

70749775R00018